GENTLE WILLOW
A Story for Children About Dying

by Joyce C. Mills, Ph.D.

illustrated by Michael Chesworth

Magination Press • Washington, DC

to all of the butterflies
who dance in many ways
to all my relations
Joyce

Library of Congress Cataloging-in-Publication Data
Mills, Joyce C.,
    Gentle Willow : a story for children about dying / by Joyce C.
Mills : illustrated by Michael Chesworth.
        p.   cm.
    Summary: Amanda is upset that she is going to lose her friend
Gentle Willow, but the Tree Wizards help her understand that her
memories are gifts from her friend and that there are special ways
of saying goodbye.
    ISBN 0-945354-54-1 (cloth). — ISBN 0-945354-53-3 (paper)
    1. Trees—Fiction. 2. Death—Fiction.]   I. Chesworth,
Michael,
ill. II. Title.
PZ7.M63977Ge   1993
[E]—dc20   93-22770
                                                          CIP
                                                           AC

Manufactured in the United States of America

10 9 8 7 6 5 4 3

Introduction for Parents

Death and dying are difficult subjects for us as adults to deal with ourselves, let alone explain to children. Also, while it is one thing to explain the death of an older person, such as a grandparent, who has lived a full life, it is quite another to try to explain to a child the death of someone young, perhaps the same age as the child. It can be harder still to talk about death with a child who is him- or herself living with a life-threatening illness.

As adults we search for the meaning of illnesses, such as cancer or AIDS, that shorten the precious life of a child. Children who face, and children who are living with, life-threatening illnesses have many questions themselves: Why is it happening to me? Why does my friend have to die? We may have ideas or beliefs about the best way to talk with children about these important questions. And we may also look for extra help or another way of telling the story.

Born out of the inspirational story of *Little Tree,* a healing story for children who face serious medical problems, *Gentle Willow* was written for children who may not survive their illness, and for the children who know them. This loving and tender story brings back the characters of Little Tree, Amanda the squirrel, and the two tree wizards, Fixumup and Imageen, to address feelings of disbelief, anger and sadness along with love, compassion and care-giving. *Gentle Willow* provides children, and those who are reading the story with them, a "transformational" way of viewing death and dying.

We all recognize that the greatest loss a parent can experience is the loss of a child. As parents or caregivers we feel helpless when we are unable to effect a "cure" for our children. The story of *Gentle Willow* reminds us that although we may not have the medical "cures" as yet for many illnesses that affect the bodies of our children, we can still provide a loving atmosphere in which "healing" can occur on an emotional and spiritual level of life. . .and that stories and love are the healing medicines of the human soul.

It was the time of Spring once again, when all the flowers bloomed their brightest colors. It had been a long time since the big storm came through the forest where Little Tree and her friend Amanda lived and played.

Since that time, many new friends had come to live in the forest. Little Tree and Amanda especially liked Gentle Willow, who lived across the pond. Each day as the sun rose in the East, Little Tree rustled her leaves and sang "Good Morning" to her friends.

Each day Gentle Willow invited the wind to blow through her branches, creating a sound like crystal chimes, to say "Good Morning" back.

Amanda liked playing with Gentle Willow. Her new friend gave her places to store her nuts.

Amanda also liked to chase the big yellow butterflies who danced within Gentle Willow's long and graceful branches.

One day, while Amanda was climbing up the trunk of Gentle Willow, she noticed that her friend looked different. Her bark was lumpy and bumpy. Her leaves were turning brown, and her branches were droopy.

"What is wrong, Gentle Willow?" asked Amanda.

"I don't know," whispered Gentle Willow. "I just feel different."

"Don't worry," said Amanda. "Tomorrow you will feel better."

But many tomorrows came, and Gentle Willow still did not feel better.

Amanda was worried. She ran around the pond and told Little Tree about their friend.

"Remember when the big storm came and I was hurt?" asked Little Tree.

"Yes!" cried Amanda. "And Fixumup and Imageen came and fixed your broken branches. I'll go get them. Maybe they can help Gentle Willow, too."

The two tree wizards came at Amanda's call.

Fixumup checked Gentle Willow's branches and her lumpy, bumpy bark. Imageen looked closely at her roots. Amanda stayed close. The butterflies danced all around Gentle Willow, while Little Tree watched from across the pond.

After all the checking, Imageen and Fixumup went to the knowing rock by the pond to talk. Amanda followed.
"What is wrong with Gentle Willow?" she asked.

"Your friend's hurt is different from the hurt Little Tree had because of the storm," said Fixumup. "Gentle Willow has something we have seen before in the forest, but we cannot make it go away."

"What do you mean?" Amanda yelled. "You HAVE to help Gentle Willow. You HAVE to make her better. YOU ARE THE TREE WIZARDS OF THE FOREST!"

"Yes," said Imageen sadly, "we are Tree Wizards. But there are some things even Tree Wizards cannot fix. We can give Gentle Willow tree sap to help her feel stronger. We can give her herbs to help her feel comfortable. But we cannot make her all better."

"What will happen to her?" asked Amanda.

"Gentle Willow will look different as time goes by," said Imageen. "She will need all of our help every day. We can sing her songs and tell her stories. Each of our songs and each of our stories will help her feel a special medicine called Love."

Amanda, Fixumup and Imageen went together to tell Little Tree about Gentle Willow.

"We are losing our friend," cried Little Tree. "What will we do without her?"

"You are right, Little Tree," said Imageen. "You won't know or see Gentle Willow as you know her now. She is going on a journey of changing forms. Human people call it dying. But all the years you have known Gentle Willow, she has been giving you special gifts."

"Gifts?" asked Amanda and Little Tree.

"Yes. Special gifts called memories. Memories of her crystal
chimes. . .memories of waving good morning. . .memories of
laughing with the wind. . .memories of special times you've
shared together. The time will come when all of us who live in
the forest will sing a special song to say 'Goodbye' to Gentle
Willow as we know her today. And the time will come when
we will recognize her in another way. Maybe it will be in a song
from the wind. Maybe it will be in the dance of the butterflies. I
don't know. But each of you will know in your own special way."

Every day Little Tree looked across the pond and rustled her leaves to sing songs to Gentle Willow. And every day Amanda visited and told her stories. One day, while Amanda was visiting, Gentle Willow began to cry.

"I am afraid to change. I want to stay the way I am. I want to stay a tree."

Not knowing how to help her friend, Amanda sat quietly. She just listened, and stayed close, while Gentle Willow wept. Then Amanda remembered about songs and stories. . .and love. As she was trying to think of a good story, one of the big yellow butterflies fluttered by. Amanda snuggled closer to Gentle Willow and began her story.

"Once a long time ago, when Yellow Butterfly was little, she was something called a caterpillar. She was fuzzy and long and crawled on the ground, over rocks and flowers.

"After a while, Yellow Butterfly felt something inside her changing. But she did not know what the change would be.

"She grew tired and needed to rest. That is how she came to you, Gentle Willow. She needed a branch to rest upon.

"Butterfly began to spin a warm blanket around herself. Inside of the blanket it was verrrry dark. Yellow Butterfly felt her whole fuzzy caterpillar self changing shape.

"After what seemed a very long time, she felt ready to come out of the blanket. She did not want to be in that darkness anymore.

"So, using all her strength, Yellow Butterfly pushed herself out into the light.

"And there she was.

"Not crawling on the ground anymore. . .not a fuzzy caterpillar anymore. Instead, she had silken yellow wings. Her whole form had changed. And, as she flew, she found all the other butterflies just like herself."

When Amanda finished the story, she noticed that Gentle
Willow had stopped crying. She seemed to be smiling a quiet
understanding.

It was the time of Spring once again, when all the flowers bloomed their brightest colors. Little Tree and Amanda looked across the pond to the place where Gentle Willow once stood.

"Look," said Little Tree. "The big yellow butterflies have come back to dance."

"Yes," said Amanda. "Perhaps, in a different way, they still hear the crystal songs of our friend Gentle Willow."

My Pain Getting Better Book

Children who are living with life-threatening illnesses often experience both pain and fear. We have learned that imagery can be a powerful tool to help children feel more in control of their physical and emotional discomfort. The **My Pain Getting Better Book** exercise is a simple, and fun, technique that parents or other caregivers can offer children in or out of the hospital.

It starts by giving your child a drawing pad or three sheets of paper along with crayons or markers. Ask your child to:

1. Draw a picture of the pain or fear.
2. Draw how that picture (#1) looks feeling "all better."
3. Draw what will change picture #1 into picture #2.

These three simple steps help children separate from pain or fear and call upon their inner "healing helpers" to create a symbol of "all better" or relief.

The **Magic Happy Breath** exercise can further expand and deepen your child's comfort. Ask your child to close his or her eyes, take a nice, deep, slow breath in through the nose and out through the mouth, as if gently blowing a feather. Next, ask your child to imagine picture #3 going inside, right to the place of the hurt or afraid feeling, until it is changed into picture #2, the "all better" picture.

For example: If your child's first drawing is a scribbley line, the second picture a rainbow, and the third picture a heart, say to your child, "Close your eyes and watch the heart as it goes all the way to the scribbley line. When the scribble (pain or fear) changes to the rainbow, open your eyes and enjoy seeing your rainbow."

RELATED BOOKS FROM MAGINATION PRESS:

Gran-Gran's Best Trick: A Story for Children Who Have Lost Someone They Love, by L. Dwight Holden (1989).

Little Tree: A Story for Children with Serious Medical Problems, by Joyce C. Mills (1992).

Sammy's Mommy Has Cancer, by Sherry Kohlenberg (1993).

The Three Birds: A Story for Children About the Loss of a Loved One, by Marinus van den Berg (1994).

To order, call 1-800-374-2721.